I0669851

Samuel Smith, Charles Ira Bushnell

Memoirs of Samuel Smith

A Soldier of the Revolution, 1776-1786

Samuel Smith, Charles Ira Bushnell

Memoirs of Samuel Smith
A Soldier of the Revolution, 1776-1786

ISBN/EAN: 9783337133528

Printed in Europe, USA, Canada, Australia, Japan

Cover: Foto ©Raphael Reischuk / pixelio.de

More available books at **www.hansebooks.com**

GENERAL SULLIVAN

MEMOIRS

OF

SAMUEL SMITH,

A

SOLDIER OF THE REVOLUTION,

1776-1786,

WRITTEN BY HIMSELF.

WITH

A PREFACE AND NOTES.

BY

CHARLES I. BUSHNELL.

NEW YORK:
PRIVATELY PRINTED.
1860.

Entered, according to Act of Congress, in the year 1860, by

CHARLES I. BUSHNELL,

In the Clerks' Office of the District Court of the United States, for the Southern District of New York.

PREFACE.

THE following work was originally published in Middleborough, Mass., in the year 1853, and the very small edition that was printed was chiefly circulated by the Author among such inhabitants of that town as had befriended him, or of whom he solicited alms.

Though but the memoirs of a private soldier, and of unpretending character, yet it is one of several similar ones extant, showing the trials undergone and the privations and sufferings endured by our ancestors in their noble contest for freedom.

Samuel Smith, the author of the Memoirs, was for several years in the habit of annually visiting the city of New Bedford, and participating in the municipal celebrations on the Fourth of July. At the visit he made preceding his death, his mind was still unimpaired, and he was in the full possession of his physical strength. He died in the town of Middleborough, on Friday, July 7th, 1854, in the 95th year of his age.

INTRODUCTION.

~~~~~~~~~~~~

I HAVE contemplated for several years, placing before the American people, a few pages detailing some of the many incidents of my early life, my birth, parentage, and entrance into the army of the American Revolution, in 1776, &c., &c. Hoping that a recital of those labors, hardships, sufferings and trials may be kindly received by my fellow-countrymen, with a hearty response to the demand which I make upon them, namely : a perusal of these few pages, and the payment solicited for the same.

SAMUEL SMITH.

Middleboro', Mass., May, 1853.

MEMOIRS.

I WAS born in Smithfield,* in Rhode Island, on the 13th of June, A.D. 1759, of humble, creditable parents. My early education was exceedingly limited, never having attended school but two winters, and in that time barely learned to read some easy lessons without spelling, and to write the letters of the alphabet with a copy.

When eight years old, I was afflicted with a fever sore, which entirely disabled me for a year, and prevented my ever having full use of my right arm.

My mother died when I was about thirteen years old, and I was taken into the family of a friendly man, with whom I remained one year, receiving as a compensation for my work, necessary clothing and board. At the expiration of that time, I went to live with a bachelor, agreeing to stay three years, as at the former place,

* A town in Providence Co., on the Pawtucket River, six miles from Providence.

namely, for victuals and clothes. After being with him one and a half years, I was, like many foolish boys, enticed away by a stranger, and told by him that he would do better by me than the person with whom I then resided—that he wished me to drive team, &c. In consequence of this flattery and deception, I ran away from the bachelor, and joined my new acquaintance.

In three weeks, however, I returned, and begged the privilege of staying, which was granted.

At the expiration of three years, I hired myself again to him one year, for necessary clothing and twelve dollars. The next year I was paid fifteen dollars and clothes ; then my master relinquished house-keeping, and I was again destitute of a home. My parents being both dead, I was in a lonely condition, but was kindly cared for, and during a long illness which now prostrated me, carefully watched over by a widow, who was, indeed, to me like a " guardian angel." She also read and explained to me many passages of Scripture, which I did not before understand, and could not read for myself.

Soon after I regained my strength, there was a call for soldiers to go to Bristol, and many were drafted to go there. I was hired for one month to take a soldier's place. When that time expired, I enlisted for three months, and when that time was served, I again enlisted in the Continental Army, but was never mustered as a soldier, on account of my right arm being shorter than my left.

About this time a small party of recruits were detached from the forces at Bristol, to join the main army. I was one of the number. We joined the main army in the Highlands, on the east side of Hudson River, opposite Stony Point.*

Soon after we joined the main army, Major Andre (1) was brought into camp, and continued in the regiment till he was hung.† From the Highlands we marched to " Red Bank,"(2) where we had a severe battle with the Hessians.

In this engagement they attempted several times to storm our fort, there being seven times as many Hessians as our number. They were, however, compelled to retreat. In this engagement we had one captain, one fife major, and five privates killed. Two of the privates were shot down, one on my right and the other on my left hand.

---

* A promontory on the west side of the Hudson River, near the entrance of the Highlands, famous for the strength of its fortifications, which were successfully stormed by Gen. Wayne on the 15th day of July, 1779.

† The reader will perceive that the author is guilty of several anachronisms in the course of his narrative.

For notes indicated by figures thus (1), see Appendix.

The night following the battle we were all on duty, either in scouting parties or on trails. It fell to my lot to go with a party on trail, and in going about half gun shot from the fort we found Count Dnnop(3) wounded and concealed behind a pine, attended by his two waiters. We took him and carried him into the fort. He lived but a short time and died of his wounds, having been shot through the knees with small grape-shot. The next day the whole regiment was employed, except those on guard and on scouting parties, in digging a ' trench and burying the dead. Here we buried between four and five hundred ; so many Hessians having fallen in the engagement.

Having buried the dead, we hung three spies—one white man and two negroes. The white man confessed that he had taken pay of the British, (a tankard full of guineas,) for conducting Hessians to Red Bank.

Soon after this action the British shipping came up opposite a mud fort which we had built, and another action commenced. We succeeded, soon after the action commenced, in firing a red hot shot into one of their ships, the Roebuck, a ship of seventy-four guns, which connecting with her magazine, blew her up.

Sometime in November, 1776, we were obliged to leave Red Bank on account of the cold, and we marched to Valley Forge, and again joined the main army—being at this time nearly destitute of clothing, except what we secured in the Hessian fight. We stopped, however, sometime in the mountains, till we could procure provisions. We there visited a hermit, who was one of the oldest settlers, having lived forty miles in the wild wilderness for fifty years. As the regiment was passing the cabin of the hermit, the column halted, and there was liberty given for all to visit it. It was a nice cabin, furnished with furs and skins. A nice smooth bench set outside the door. About two rods from this cabin, to the right hand as we came out, stood a very large tree, with smooth bark, resembling poplar. On this tree was nicely pictured a warrior's face. There were days while we were on our march to Valley Forge, for winter quarters, that we were entirely destitute of food, sometimes two days at a time. On our march we came to a valley, which abounded with black walnuts and butternuts, where we tarried two days. We then continued our march till we came to the Schuylkill River. There we laid down to rest on our arms, with nothing but the broad canopy of heaven to cover us. That night the snow fell about half a foot deep. Some had blankets and slept upon the frozen ground and covered themselves with them, while others had none, and

slept entirely unprotected from the weather. We staid
at this place two days. The second day, in the morning,
we discovered near the camp a large flock of goats,
which were taken, butchered and devoured to satisfy
hunger. After two days we unloaded the baggage
wagons, and hauled them into the river to make a bridge
on which the regiment crossed. On the next march we
suffered extremely, our feet being wet, and being
compelled to travel on the wet, frozen ground, ice
and snow. Those who had blankets cut off the corners
and wound them round their feet. Others who had
none, secured rags and the like, or anything of the kind
which had been thrown from the houses on the road
on which we marched, and blood from our feet might
be traced on the ground. We finally reached Valley
Forge, our winter head-quarters, the forepart of January,
1777. Here I built a hut, and soon after finishing it,
was taken sick, and was blind for about ten days. We
remained at Valley Forge till sometime in June. Then
we went out of our winter quarters into the fields with
our tents, and marched from post to post till we met the
British at Springfield,(4)Penn., where we had a smart engagement, lasting for nearly two hours.* There be
ing of us but a small brigade to contend against the

* The Battle of Springfield took place on the 23d day of June, 1780.

whole British army, we were obliged for a time, in this action to retreat, and a company was detached from our brigade, in a flanking party, and attacked the British right flank opposite General Arnold's, the traitor.

We contended in this engagement nearly an hour, until in fact the British had nearly surrendered to us, when we were obliged to retreat a short distance on a height of ground and took shelter, first in an orchard and from thence we retreated to an oak grove. Here we had the advantage of them. Our captain now ordered every man to shelter himself by standing behind a tree. In this engagement there was not a man on the American side killed or wounded except one captain, who received a shot through the left arm ; a flesh wound.

The next day after the battle, we were employed in burying the dead in the burying ground, and conveying the wounded to the hospital. I was selected with others to go to the hospital and attend the wounded. Much of my time while there was employed in attending and waiting on the doctor, having the care of his box of instruments. While there I saw a great many legs and arms cut off. I was continued in this occupation at the hospital, until the spring of 1778, when I joined my regiment again.

While I was at the hospital I was under the command of the doctor, and I waited on him until he left the army, which was in the fall of the year 1778. The name of the doctor was Elias Cornelius.(5.)

I believe him to have been a Christian, as he regularly attended meetings on Sundays. He was a Baptist by profession. When he went to church he always took me with him, as he wished me well. He also instructed me in the ways of righteousness. When he left the army I lost the company of my best friend. He returned from Springfield to his home in the city of New York. After the British took possession of New York, he was obliged to leave the city, he being a true Republican. His father and relatives were Tories. The last knowledge I had of him, he resided at Robinson Mills, in the State of New York, and the last time I saw him he was on a visit to Providence, two years after he left the army, when we took a final leave of each other. He entreated me to persevere in serving the Lord, that we might meet in a better world.

Nothing material occurred until the next June, when the battle of Monmouth (6) was fought. The day on which this battle was fought, was the hottest, I think, that I ever experienced. In fact, the heat was so excessive that I could not tell by which the most died, whether by the heat or the balls.

In two days after this hot battle, the brigade was ordered to march to Rhode Island.(7.) We arrived on the Island just previous to the tremendous hurricane and rain storm. We had not pitched our tents. I found, however, a large hogshead, knocked in at one end, and got into it for shelter. Soon after the storm, an action took place. In this action the Americans were obliged to retreat. It so happened that it brought the Rhode Island brigade in the rear. Boats were employed all night in carrying off baggage and troops. About sunrise it came our turn to fight, and we descended upon a party of British at the fort on Butts Hill. The British scaled the walls on one side, while the Americans entered the gate.

We drove the British completely from the fort, dismounted and spiked their cannon, and then hastened to the boats which were waiting for us, and retreated from the Island.

Soon after, the drafted men were discharged, and we marched to Warren* for winter headquarters. The soldiers called for pay. They had had promises of pay for one month in the new emission money. The money was retained by our officers, and we marched to Providence

* A town in Bristol Co., R. I., at the mouth of Palmer's River, eleven miles from Providence.

to see the General and get redress, which he promised
we should have, and told our commander whenever we
wanted redress, to write him, and he would endeavor
that we should have it, so we all again submitted, and
resigned ourselves to the orders of our old officers.

In the course of the winter of 1778, many of the regiment to which I belonged were taken to go on ship
board, to run down the river to attack and take the
British shipping which lay there. The ship that I went
on board of had two cannons Our orders were to run
along side of the British shipping, board, and take them.

I believe it was a happy incident to us that our captain run the ship aground on Pawtucket Flats, for thus
ended this expedition. We then returned to our bar-
racks at Warren, where we remained until the spring
of the year 1779, when we were marched to Boston
Neck.

Our payment for services being unnecessarily detain-
ed, we all agreed to have a letter formed, setting forth
our grievances, and sent to our General.(8). The letter
was made and handed to the Colonel to forward to the
General. The Colonel refused to have the letter sent,
and took the bearer of it and sent him in irons to jail.
He then had him tried by a Court Martial, and sentenced
to be hung in five days. Three days after the sentence,

all attended as usual at the calling of the roll. After the roll was called we were dismissed for the day. When the officers had retired, we agreed upon our plan to liberate the prisoner. Every soldier fixed his bayonet on his gun for the purpose of rescuing the brother soldier who was condemned to be hung. The drums beat the long roll as a signal. Every soldier was on parade, with his gun loaded and his bayonet affixed. We were determined to rescue the prisoner, who was innocent of any crime on behalf of his fellow soldiers. We were determined to a man to lose our lives or rescue our brother.

There were but two officers in the regiment who would allow soldiers to converse with our head commander, for the purpose of settling questions in dispute. On we marched, agreed that fifteen only should be allowed to settle the affair. Meeting General Sullivan, he ordered us to halt, but we marched steadily on. Our old Major, whom we always and at all times authorized to speak to our Commander to settle questions and restore peace, rode in front of our ranks and wished us to halt, as Gen. Sullivan came to settle the disorder and to restore peace. We agreed to halt on condition that the officers should get in front, under the muzzles of our guns. These conditions were quickly complied with. The first request of the General was for us to lay down our arms. He said he could not converse with soldiers under arms. We positively refused to accede to his request, and we all stood with our guns to our shoulders, loaded and bayonets affixed.

The above took place in the road on a low piece of land. A small island was opposite the place where we halted. The General wanted us to march on the island. We complied with his request. When we had marched on the island, he wanted we should stack our arms. Our leader told the General that our arms would remain in each man's hands until the treaty which we demanded was agreed upon. The General said he could not agree with soldiers upon anything while they were under arms. Then our leader told him he should march for the condemned man. The General told him that he had one black regiment in the fort, which we had to pass, who would cut us to pieces. The answer from our leader was : "We do not fear you, with all your black boys ! The prisoner we will have, at the risk of our lives !"

The General then agreed that if we would march back, under order to our former officers, he would send the prisoner to the camp. This our leader refused to do, telling the General that he had marched his men there on conditions, and that he would march them back again if he would immediately deliver up the prisoner, and pledge his honor that there should be no one confined or tried in Court Martial for the same offence. It was apparently hard for the General to agree to it, but at last he complied with the terms and sent an officer for the prisoner, who was soon brought and delivered to us. We then marched to our old encampment with our comrade in the centre, and colors flying in his hands, and resigned ourselves to our old officers.

We remained in our encampment until the British evacuated Rhode Island, when we took possession of it.* We remained here until we had orders to march southward.

The first march we made was to Hartford, Conn., where we staid but a day or two, when we marched to Philadelphia, Penn., where we encamped a week or more, waiting for further orders and for the baggage to come up. We then marched to the head of Elk River, and took boats and went down the river to Little York. Then came on a squall, and being in flat bottom boats, all landed on an island nearly opposite Little York, in the centre of the British forces. The enemy might have taken with ease the whole of the American troops which

* The British evacuated Rhode Island on the 25th of October, 1779.

were there quartered, and all our baggage, had they dared to have attacked us. One British boat landed about a mile from our encampment, and sent out spies who fled before we could come up with them. It being a pleasant day we took to our boats and sailed by them.

The next march we made was to Yorktown, where we encamped within half cannon shot of the British, and commenced a fortification by digging a trench, or rather by each man digging a hole deep enough to drop into. When this was accomplished, we stationed a man to watch the enemy's guns, at which every man dropped into his hole. But we soon left this ground, and in the night stormed two of their fortifications, and dug a trench all round the British encampment, completely yarding them in.

Two nights after the storming of the fortifications, the British undertook to retake them, and mustering out a small party calling themselves Americans, came up in the rear of us. They entered the fort with but little difficulty, as there were but few of us in it, and very quickly those who were not instantly killed or taken, were driven out of it.

Four days from that time Lord Cornwallis surrendered,(9) and in three days from the time Cornwallis surrendered, the British marched out on the plains, and stacked their arms and resigned and surrendered themselves prisoners of war, and each marched into town again. The Americans followed them. In three weeks from the time the British surrendered, we took their shipping.

Forty of the prisoners we took from their ships had a disorder with which our doctor was not acquainted. Its appearance was sudden. Some would fall down on the deck and froth like a mad dog ; others would begin to draw their heads down till their heels and head would touch together. An American of my acquaintance, who, to my certain knowledge, had been exposed repeatedly to the small pox for six years, caught it on board the British shipping and died.

From York Town we marched to Saratoga, a long and tedious march, where we made our headquarters until the spring of 1783.

In the winter, after the lakes had frozen up, we went to storm a fort on the frontier. Our army was conveyed in stages. In crossing Niagara River on the ice, just above the Falls, one stage containing six men and the driver, slipped sideways into the river, and was carried over the Falls and lost.

We passed over across the Lake to a piece of swampy land, where the stages left us and returned home. We staid here two nights and a part of two days, when we

learned by our spies, that the British had reënforced
their fort with double the number of men they had before, and it becoming more than five degrees colder
than when we started from Saratoga to cross the Lakes
—a number of men having frozen to death, and a great
part of the regiment being more or less frozen—but little
regard was paid to the command of the officers, as every
man did the best he could to protect himself from the
cold. Sleighs were procured and furnished by the inhabitants, to carry the troops back to Saratoga. We
remained at Saratoga until the latter part of the month
of May, 1783, when the greater part of the regiment was
disbanded by companies. Some of the companies were
marched to Providence before their discharge was given
them.

I was selected to drive the Colonel's baggage to
Providence, under command of a lieutenant and a small
guard, and then discharged without money or clothes.

I went to a place to board, but having no money to
pay, the person with whom I boarded set me to driving
trucks. The business he was in was small, and he entered into company with Samuel Bagley. I was finally
hired to drive a baggage wagon from Providence to
Boston. They agreed to give me one-third of the profits
for driving, I to find myself. Bagley was agent, and

about six months after I commenced driving, he sold what little property he had and ran away with the money. In consequence of this, I lost the whole of my earnings.

I then shipped on board a brig, which was bound to the coast of Brazil, on a whaling voyage. We were gone nine months and seventeen days. We killed only five whales, which made sixty barrels each, (300). I lost my time, and was in debt for fitting out.

In four days after my arrival home, I shipped for the West Indies, in a brig commanded by Capt. Seth Wheaton. Here I began a wickedness beyond every thing I had done before. In those days sailors were addicted to drinking and swearing. I contracted the habit of swearing, but not that of drinking, and did not follow all the sailors' practices, being careful of the company I kept.

The voyage was long and tedious, as the captain chartered his brig to a merchant in New York to go to Turks Island(10) and load with salt. After we had arrived at Mooner Passage,(11) we attempted to go through a narrow place, and the wind being ahead we had a very narrow escape.

After we got to sea, we were very scant of provisions, calculating to obtain supplies at Turks Island. Being

eighteen days from Curago,* we were nearly destitute
of bread and water, and four days previous to arriving
at Turks Island, were obliged to come on an allowance
of half a pint of water and half a biscuit a day. We
were, however, at this point, nearly in sight of Port au
Prince,(12) but did not dare to go on shore with our
boats. When we came so nigh to land that we could
go on shore and return in five hours, our boat was hoist-
ed out, and the captain, merchant, three sailors and myself, left the vessel about 7 o'clock, A. M., and pulled for
the shore till 3 o'clock, P. M., and reached the land.
The captain and merchant went in pursuit of provisions ;
the rest were left with me to take care of the boat.
Very soon after we landed, a negro came to the boat
with bananas, plantains and oranges to sell. We pur-
chased enough to make a good meal. The captain and
merchant soon returned with a supply of provisions,
which were brought to the boat by negroes. At five
o'clock, P. M., we pulled again for the brig. The light
which we left burning in the morning and hanging in
the shrouds, the mate put out after dark, and the wind
blowing in shore, we made sail and run for the harbor.

* Curaçoa, an island in the Caribbean Sea, 30 miles long and 10 broad.
Its chief town is Curaçoa. The principal products of the island are sugar
and tobacco.

A man-of-war, not finding the captain, and only the mate, two hands and one passenger on board, and taking her to be a pirate, brought the brig under his stern. When the light was put out, we put the boat about for the shore, it being exceedingly dark, and we had no compass. We again reached the land, and passed the remainder of the night in the small village where we had obtained our supplies. The next morning the brig was not to be seen, and we had to take to our boat again, and row across the bay, sixty miles to the harbor. We pulled all day, and at sunset were barely in sight of the shipping. When it became so dark that we could not discern the shipping, the captain selected a star in the horizon, and thus we reached the harbor about ten o'clock. As we approached the shipping, our boat was hailed by the sentinel of the man-of-war and ordered along side. Our captain was ordered on board, but in a short time was liberated, with provisions and water, to go on board of his own vessel.

We staid in port about two weeks till the merchant had taken his cargo, and then sailed for New York, where we arrived in ten days; discharged our cargo, and then sailed for Providence. On our passage down the Sound we experienced a heavy gale, and being in light ballast, were forced to make the nearest harbor, which was a cove on Long Island, where we laid for four days. Then we sailed out into the Sound, and it becoming perfectly calm, were floated about for four days longer, not making headway enough for steerage, being driven backwards and forwards with the tide. This was in the latter part of December, 1785, and the weather was piercing cold. After we had been becalmed four days, the wind blew a heavy gale, and we ran into New London, where we laid five days. On the sixth day, the weather proving favorable, we sailed again for Providence. The wind hauling to the eastward, began again to blow, and we steered for a small harbor on Long Island, where we staid three days. Again we sailed and arrived at Newport. The next day we sailed for Providence, and after contending and forcing our way through the ice, arrived three miles below the town in *twenty-one* days from New York.

Arriving in Providence, I went to my old boarding-house and staid three days, when I shipped and went on board of a sloop bound to the West Indies. The crew consisted of captain, mate and four hands—all drunkards except a lad of about eighteen years and myself. We had on board ten oxen.

We cleared from Providence in the morning, in a rain storm. By nine, P. M., Block Island was two leagues astern of us,* and all hands below, drunk. It was blowing a heavy gale, and I had been placed at the helm before leaving the land. It became dark, and not knowing the bearings of Nantucket Shoals, neither had I time to look in any book or on any chart to ascertain. I placed the lad at the helm while I went into the steerage and took the stopples out of the kegs of rum and let it run out on the floor. The two hands came on deck the next morning sober and continued so till our arrival at the West Indies. The captain and mate kept half drunk the whole voyage. They were not even capable of managing the vessel, or of discharging or loading. The mate staid on board a sloop loading with sugar, while we were loading. When we hauled out into deep water to sail for home, the captain was hardly capable of giving orders. At five o'clock, P. M., he gave me the charge of the vessel, calling all hands and ordering them to obey my orders the same as if I were the captain, and then went below. About eight o'clock the next morning he again made his appearance on deck, ordered the boat alongside, and then two hands to row him on shore. It being Sunday I kept all hands on board Monday morning the captain came on board in a negro boat,

* An island belonging to the State of Rhode Island. It is 7 miles long by 4 wide, and is 24 miles from Newport.

and gave all hands liberty to go on shore to spend the day.

We staid in port two weeks, loaded with cotton and sugar, and cleared for Providence. We had a very pleasant voyage home, except with our captain and mate, who were very cross and ugly. The captain and myself had a few words one day, and I informed him that I knew my duty as a seaman. He ever after on the voyage, appeared to owe me a grudge. A few days out, our studding sail halyards gave way at the end of the boom where it was rigged out at the end of the yard. The captain called upon me to go aloft and reef the halyards. There was no foot rope to rest the feet upon, but I had to crawl out on the yard with the halyards in my hand. When I had got about half way out, the captain sung out with an oath : " Now fall overboard, and I will pick you up when I come this way again." I was obliged to cling to the spar to the utmost of my strength, and had it not been for the stillness of the wind and the smoothness of the sea, should have fallen off.

We had a moderate breeze on our passage home till we made Block Island. The wind being to the north we could not run to Rhode Island, but anchored off Stonington, where we remained three days. In weighing anchor, we did not get it to the cat-head as quick as the captain wished, he (being so intoxicated he did not know what he wanted,) began to curse and swear, directing foul language towards me, saying were he nigh some desolate island, I should starve to death. I informed him that I had ever done my duty as a faithful seaman, and obeyed all his commands. He frequently quarreled with the mate and all hands.

I sailed the vessel from our anchorage in Stonington* to Providence. About half way from Newport to Providence, I called the captain, he having slept his nap out.

Having discharged the cargo, I called for my pay, which was six dollars a month, and the captain offered me a kind of paper currency (13) which the State had issued as a cheat. I refused this currency. He declared I should take that or nothing. I lost my wages.

Next day I visited a brother, five miles in the country, whom I found ploughing, it being a very warm time in the spring of 1786.

Upon revisiting Boston, I shipped on board a Plymouth packet. Subsequently I sailed on another voyage to the West Indies, and upon returning from which I came to Middleboro', where I have resided for about thirty-seven years, with a less varied life than that

* A seaport town in New London County, Connecticut.

which is recounted in the foregoing pages, and from
which place this little work is submitted.

Having touched in these few pages, on some of the
incidents of my younger years, I most humbly beg to ar-
rest your attention one moment longer.

FELLOW COUNTRYMEN : I need not tell you that I have
seen the British guns fired in anger, or that these lungs
which now but feebly respire the vital air of heaven,
have been suffocated with the smoke of British powder.
I need not tell you that those dim eyes have guided, or
that those now palsied limbs have directed the American
ordnance, when your country groaned, and Americans
bled by the cruel oppression of Britain.   I need not tell
you that these ears have been stunned by the thunder
of the cannon, the clashing of steel, and rattle of mus-
ketry, or even that I have lived, not only in the days
but with our beloved Washington, the father of his
country ! No ! it is not to impose upon you self-praise,
or to arouse your passions by a recital of any exertions
of my own, in behalf of the American Revolution, or even
again to revert to those times which tried men's souls, but
merely to say, gentlemen, I am an old man—a very old
man—more than four-score years and ten, and stand

nigh the borders of the grave ! I can speak to you but a short time longer. Hear me for my cause !

Should our country, in your time, be invaded by a foreign foe, and you be called to act the part of men— American born men—may you enter the field, and should it be ordered and ordained that your bones should bleach in the soil of your country, like those who fell in the American Revolution—may you say—" Let justice be done, though the heavens should fall."

NOTES.

(1) Major Andre was captured on the 23d day of September, 1780, by three militia-men, named John Paulding, David Williams, and Isaac Van Wart. He was tried by a board of general officers, of which Major Gen. Green was president, and sentenced to be hung as a spy. The sentence was carried into effect at Tappan, N. Y., on the 2d day of Oct. following. In the year 1821, the remains of Andre were disinterred and carried to England, by royal mandate, and buried in Westminster Abbey, where a monument was erected to his memory. The fate of Andre has been the subject of much lamentation. The fact, however, of his having previously acted the part of a spy at the siege of Charleston, detracts greatly from the general sympathy he would otherwise receive.

> See Johnson's Life of Gen Green, vol. 1, p. 209.
> Johnson's Traditions of the Rev., p. 255.
> Vindication of the Captors.

(2) For the security of Philadelphia, on the east side, the Americans, besides preparing gallies, floating batteries, armed vessels and boats, fire ships and rafts, had built a fort on Mud

Island, on the Delaware, about seven miles below Philadelphia, which they called Fort Mifflin, and another at Red Bank, nearly opposite on the Jersey shore, which they called Fort Mercer. A detachment from the British army having dislodged the Americans from Billingsport, where a fortification had also been made, batteries were erected by them on the Pennsylvania shore to assist in dislodging them also from Mud Island. A detachment was sent at the same time to attack Fort Mercer. This enterprise was entrusted to Col. Count Dunop, a brave and highly spirited German officer, who, with three battalions of Hessian grenadiers, the regiment of Mirback, and the infantry chasseurs, having crossed the Delaware from Philadelphia, on the 21st of October, 1777, marched down on the eastern side of the river, and on the afternoon of the next day reached Red Bank. The place was defended by about 400 men, under the command of Lieut. Col. Christopher Greene, of Rhode Island. Count Dunop, with undaunted firmness, led on his troops to the assault, through a tremendous fire, and forcing an extensive outwork, compelled the garrison to retire to the redoubt, but while fighting bravely at the head of his battalion he received a mortal wound. The assailants were soon forced to a precipitate retreat under a well-directed fire from the garrison, which again proved destructive to them as it had previously been in their approach to the assault. In this expedition the enemy was supposed to have lost about 400 men. The garrison lost thirty-two only, killed and wounded. The garrison at Red Bank was, however, afterwards withdrawn on the approach of Cornwallis with a large force. The fort at Mud Island was also finally abandoned by the Americans, thereby leaving to the British an open communication between their army and fleet.

Holmes' Annals, vol. 2, p. 267.   Morse's Annals, p. 279.
Thatcher's Journal, p. 118.   Heath's Memoirs, p. 137.

Christopher Greene, the hero of Red Bank, was born in Warwick, R. I., in the year 1737. In 1775 he was a major under his relative, Gen. Nathaniel Greene. He accompanied Arnold through the wilderness. At the siege of Quebec, being in command of a company, he was taken prisoner. After his exchange, he was entrusted by Gen. Washington with the command of Fort Mercer, on the Delaware, commonly called Red Bank, where he gallantly repulsed the assault of Col. Dunop, on the 22d day of Oct., 1777. For this service Congress voted him a sword, which was presented to his eldest son in 1786. In the year 1778, Lieut. Col. Greene was with the army under Sullivan. In the spring of 1781, having been posted on Croton River, he was surprised by a corps of refugees and barbarously murdered, in the 44th year of his age.

(3) Count Dunop was a brave and gallant officer. He was considered the best officer of the Hessians, and his death was greatly lamented. While he lay upon the ground, wounded and helpless, two Hessian grenadiers attempting to carry him off the field, were shot dead under him, whereupon he entreated his men to let him remain where he was, and seek their own safety. Col. Dunop died on the 29th day of Oct., 1777, and was buried by the Americans with military honors.

(4) In the month of June, 1780, 5,000 men commanded by Lieut. Gen. Kniphausen, made an excursion from New York into New Jersey. Landing at Elizabethtown, they proceeded to Connecticut Farms, where they burned about thirteen houses and the Presbyterian church, and then proceeded to Springfield. As they advanced, they were annoyed by Col. Dayton commanding a few militia, and on their approach to the bridge near the town, they were further opposed by Gen. Maxwell, who, with a few continental troops, were prepared to dispute the passage. They made a halt, therefore, and soon after returned to Elizabethtown. Be-

fore they had retreated the whole American army at Morristown marched to oppose them. In the meantime, Sir Henry Clinton returning with his victorious troops from Charleston, ordered a re-enforcement to Kniphausen, who, with the whole body advanced a second time towards Springfield. The British were now opposed by Gen. Greene, with a considerable body of continental troops. Col. Angel with his regiment and a piece of artillery, was posted to secure the bridge. A severe action was fought, which was kept up forty minutes, after which the Americans were forced by superior numbers to retire. Gen. Greene took post with his troops on a range of hills in the hope of being attacked, but the British, having burned the town, consisting of nearly fifty dwelling houses, retreated to Elizabethtown, and the next day set out on their return to New York. The loss of the Americans in this action was about eighty; that of the British was supposed to be considerable more.

Holmes, 2, p. 315.

(5) Elias Cornelius was a native of Long Island. At the age of 19, in opposition to the advice and wishes of his relatives, who were then attached to the British cause, he repaired to New York in 1777, and being recommended by his instructor, Dr. Samuel Latham, obtained a commission as surgeon's mate in the Second Rhode Island Regiment, under command of Col. Israel Angel. On reconnoitering near the lines above New York, he was taken prisoner and carried to the old Provoost jail in the city, where he suffered incredible hardships, until with great courage and presence of mind, he made his escape in the month of March, 1778. He immediately rejoined the army, and continued in it till the close of 1781. He died at Somers, N. Y., on the 13th day of June, 1823, leaving a widow, three daughters, and a son bearing his name, who became a clergyman, was for many years connected with various religious societies, and died in 1832. As a phy-

sician, Dr. Cornelius had an extensive and successful practice. It was while in the army that he received those religious impressions which resulted in an established Christian hope. He was a warm friend to charitable institutions, and left at his decease the sum of $100 each to the American Bible Society, the Education, the Foreign Mission, and the United Foreign Mission Societies.

(6) The battle of Monmouth was fought on the 28th day of June, 1778. The loss of the Americans was 8 officers and 61 privates killed, and about 160 wounded. The loss of the British army in killed, wounded and missing, is stated to have been 358 men, including officers. About 100 were taken prisoners, and nearly 1,000 soldiers, principally foreigners, many of whom had married in Philadelphia, and deserted the British standard during the march. The victory was claimed by both parties. It is allowed that in the early part of the day the British had the advantage, but it is contended that in the latter part the advantage was on the side of the Americans, for they maintained their ground, repulsed the enemy by whom they were attacked, were prevented only by the night and the retreat of Sir Henry Clinton from renewing the action, and suffered in killed and wounded less than their adversaries.

Holmes' Annals, 2, p 255.

(7) In the month of August, 1778, an army, composed chiefly of militia and volunteers from the New England States, with two brigades of continental troops under command of Major Gen. Sullivan, laid siege to the royal army on Rhode Island. From this land force with the co-operation of the French fleet under command of Count D'Estaing, very sanguine expectations were formed that the enterprise would have been crowned with success. But the English fleet under Lord Howe appeared and Count D'Estaing was induced to pursue them and to offer battle, when

unfortunately a violent storm arose by which his fleet suffered so
considerably that the Count was obliged to quit the expedition
and proceed to Boston to repair his ships. Gen. Sullivan's army
continued several days on the island besieging the enemy, and
finally a smart engagement ensued, in which both the regular
troops and militia, emulous of fame and glory, combatted the
enemy during the day. The result of the contest was a complete
repulse of the royal forces—they retired from the field with considerable loss, and employed themselves in fortifying their camp.
In the absence of the French fleet, Sir Henry Clinton sent from
New York large re-enforcements, in consequence of which it was
unanimously agreed in a counsel of war to retire from the island.
The retreat was conducted by Gen. Sullivan with great judg-
ment and discretion, without loss of men or baggage, though in
the face of an enemy of superior force. This exploit reflected
great honor both on the General and the brave troops under his
command. In the honors of this expedition and retreat, Major
Gen. Greene and the Marquis de la Fayette participated con-
spicuously, but were greatly disappointed in the final result.

Thatcher, p. 141.

In commemoration of this masterly Bunker Hill retreat, a medal
was struck in Holland, of about one inch and a half in diameter,
bearing upon the

OB : A British man-of-war, under full sail, with colors all
   flying.
LEG : "DE ADMIRAALS FLAG VAN ADMIRAAL HOWE 1779."
      (The flag of Admiral Howe. 1779.)
REV : A representation of the retreating Americans across
      Rhode Island to their boats in waiting. On the oppo-
      site side of the island are seen three British men-of-
      war.
LEG : " D'vlugtende AMERICAANEN van RONDE YLAND Augt.
      1778."

RHODE ISLAND MEDAL.

(The flight of the Americans from Rhode Island, Augt., 1778.)

This medal, which is rarely met with, is interesting, aside from its American character, as showing the state of feeling and sympathy for the American cause at that time among the nations of Europe.

(8) John Sullivan was born in Berwick, Me., on the 17th of Jan., 1740. He was appointed by Congress a Brig. Gen. in 1775, and in 1776 a Major Gen. He superseded Arnold in the command of the army in Canada, June 4, 1776, but was soon driven out of that province. He afterwards, on the illness of Greene, took command of his division on Long Island. In the battle of Aug. 27, 1776, he was taken prisoner with Lord Sterling, but was shortly afterwards exchanged. In Augt. 22, 1777, he planned and executed an expedition against Staten Island, for which on an inquiry into his conduct he received the approbation of the Court. In September he was engaged in the battle of Brandywine, and in Oct. 4, in that of Germantown. He was afterwards detached to command the troops in Rhode Island. His gallant repulse of the enemy, and his subsequent masterly retreat have been the theme of much commendation. In the summer of 1779 he made his successful expedition against the Six Nations under Brant and others, completely dispersing them and laying waste their country. He held after the war the office of Governor of New Hampshire for several years, and in 1789 was appointed District Judge. He died in Durham, Jan'y. 28, 1795, aged 54.

(9) The surrender of Cornwallis at Yorktown, Va., took place on the 19th day of Oct., 1781. The army, with the artillery, arms, accoutrements, military chest, and all public stores, were surrendered to Gen. Washington; the ships and seamen to the Count de Grasse. The prisoners, exclusive of seamen, amounted to 7,073, of which number 5,950 were rank and file.

Garrison of York,   3.273.   Sick and wounded,   1.933
        Gloucester, 744.   4.017

Fit for duty,   4,017.   Total rank and file,   5,950
To the 7.073 prisoners are to be added 6 commissioned and 28
non-commissioned officers and privates. taken prisoners in the two
redoubts, and in the sortie made by the garrison. The loss sus-
tained by the garrison during the siege, in killed, wounded and
missing, amounted to 552. The loss of the combined army in
killed, was about 300. The allied army, to which that of Lord
Cornwallis surrendered, has been estimated at 16,000 men. The
French amounted to 7,000, the continental troops to about 5,500,
and the militia to about 3,500.

Among the general officers particularly noticed for the important services they rendered during the siege, were Gen'ls. Lincoln,
de la Fayette, Steuben, Knox and Duportail, his Excellency Count
Rochambeau, and several other French officers.

Thatcher's Journal, p. 281.
Holmes' Annals, 2, p. 333.

It is an interesting fact, though perhaps out of place here, that
Lord Cornwallis and the Marquis de la Fayette, who had fought
against each other at Yorktown, and also on several other previous occasions, met at the close of the war at the review of the
Prussian troops at Potsdam, in Prussia, in the year 1785, and
were made personally acquainted with each other through the
honorary introduction of the veteran Frederick himself.

(10) Turks' Island—one of the Bahamas. in the West Indies,
noted for the large quantity of salt made there from sea-water,
and exported to the United States and other countries.

(11) Mona Passage—a strait eighty miles across, which sepa-
rates Haiti from Porto Rico.

(12) Port au Prince is the capital city of Haiti. It has an excellent harbor and carries on a considerable trade, chiefly in sugar, coffee and indigo. It was nearly all burnt in 1791 by the revolting negroes, and was taken by the English and Royalists in 1794.

(13) The depreciation of the Rhode Island paper currency of 1786, was probably hastened by the decision of the Supreme Court of that State, in the celebrated case of Trevett vs. Weedon, at the Sept. Newport term, 1786—that the emission was unconstitutional in several important particulars. For this decision the Judges were summoned before the Assembly, and heard there by counsel, and after various debates and proceedings, they were discharged, Oct. 2d, session 1786.

See case of Trevett vs. Weedon, pub. Prov. 1787.
Potter's Rhode Island paper money, p. 19.
Chandler's Crim. Trials, 2, p. 269.

www.ingramcontent.com/pod-product-compliance
Lightning Source LLC
Chambersburg PA
CBHW021246260626
47172CB00002B/865